Welcome to ALADDIN QUIX!

If you are looking for fast, fun-to-read stories with colorful characters, lots of kid-friendly humor, easy-to-follow action, entertaining story lines, and lively illustrations, then **ALADDIN QUIX** is for you!

But wait, there's more!

If you're also looking for stories with tables of contents; word lists; about-the-book questions; 64, 80, or 96 pages; short chapters; short paragraphs; and large fonts, then **ALADDIN QUIX** is *definitely* for you!

ALADDIN QUIX: The next step between ready to reads and longer, more challenging chapter books, for readers five to eight years old.

Read more ALADDIN QUIX books!

By Stephanie Calmenson

Our Principal Is a Frog!
Our Principal Is a Wolf!
Our Principal's in His Underwear!
Our Principal Breaks a Spell!
Our Principal's Wacky Wishes!
Our Principal Is a Spider!
Our Principal Is a Scaredy-Cat!

The Adventures of Allie and Amy
By Stephanie Calmenson and Joanna Cole

Book 1: *The Best Friend Plan*
Book 2: *Rockin' Rockets*
Book 3: *Stars of the Show*

Our Principal Is a Noodlehead!

BY
Stephanie
Calmenson

ILLUSTRATED
BY Aaron
Blecha

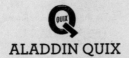

ALADDIN QUIX

New York London Toronto Sydney New Delhi

To noodleheads everywhere
—S. C.

ALADDIN QUIX
Simon & Schuster Children's Publishing Division
1230 Avenue of the Americas, New York, New York 10020
First Aladdin QUIX paperback edition August 2021
Text copyright © 2021 by Stephanie Calmenson
Illustrations copyright © 2021 by Aaron Blecha
Also available in an Aladdin QUIX hardcover edition.
All rights reserved, including the right of reproduction in whole or in part in any form.
ALADDIN and the related marks and colophon are
trademarks of Simon & Schuster, Inc.
For information about special discounts for bulk purchases, please contact
Simon & Schuster Special Sales at 1-866-506-1949 or business@simonandschuster.com.
The Simon & Schuster Speakers Bureau can bring authors to your live event. For
more information or to book an event contact the Simon & Schuster Speakers Bureau
at 1-866-248-3049 or visit our website at www.simonspeakers.com.
Designed by Karin Paprocki
The illustrations for this book were rendered digitally.
The text of this book was set in Archer Medium.
Manufactured in the United States of America 0721 OFF
2 4 6 8 10 9 7 5 3 1
Library of Congress Control Number 2021933019
ISBN 9781534479388 (hc)
ISBN 9781534479371 (pbk)
ISBN 9781534479395 (ebook)

Cast of Characters

Mr. Barnaby Bundy: Principal

Roger Patel: Top student and class leader

Mrs. Gwen Feeny: Third-grade teacher

Ms. Marilyn Moore: Assistant principal

Mr. Charles Strong: School librarian

Ms. Wanda Bly: Gym teacher

Nancy Wong: Plans to be a zoologist

Hector Gonzalez: Loves making his friends laugh

Ms. Ellie Tilly: Kindergarten teacher

Contents

Goooood Morning!

"Goooood morning, PS 88!" boomed a voice over the loud-speaker. "This is **Mr. Bundy,** and I want to wish everyone a super-duper Monday! **Three cheers for Monday!"**

All around the school, kids were giving one another looks that said, *Huh?* Their principal's morning announcements weren't usually so high-spirited.

"Mr. B's in an extra good mood today," said **Roger**.

Even his teacher, **Mrs. Feeny**, looked surprised.

After the announcement, there was a knock on Mr. Bundy's door. It was **Ms. Moore**, the assistant principal.

"Um, how are you feeling today, Mr. Bundy?" she said.

"Excellent! Absolutely excellent! How are you?" he asked.

"Pretty good," she said, feeling

as puzzled as everyone else by the principal's **behavior**. "Is this a good time to talk about next week's parent-teacher evening?"

"Yes. No. Maybe so. Can we talk tomorrow?" said Mr. Bundy.

"Ooookay," said Ms. Moore. "I was just asking since last week you said we should talk first thing Monday morning. And here we are."

"Yes, here we are, and glad of it!" said Mr. Bundy. "Now if you'll excuse me, I want to get out and make sure every-one's feeling super-duper."

"Super-duper's always good," said Ms. Moore, backing out of the office. She was feeling more puzzled by the minute.

2

Super-Duper!

As he was walking down the hall, Mr. Bundy heard voices sing out from the music room.

"Put your finger in the air, in the air.

Put your finger in the air
and leave it over there.
Put your finger in the air,
in the air!"

Mr. Bundy raised his finger in the air. Fortunately, he hadn't heard some of the kids singing, "Put your finger in your nose and see how far it goes."

Mr. Bundy's finger was still in the air when **Mr. Strong**, the librarian, came along.

"Morning, Mr. Bundy," said the

librarian. Thinking the principal was waving his finger as a greeting, Mr. Strong waved a finger back.

Just then **Ms. Bly**, the gym teacher, came down the hall, and she joined the greeting too.

The three went down the hall waving their fingers in the air, in the air. Then Mr. Strong went into the library, Ms. Bly went into the gym and Mr. Bundy continued on his way.

At the next classroom, he heard a voice call, "Feeding time!" Not realizing the student was about to feed the class hamster, the principal took his finger down from the air, grabbed a snack bar from his pocket, and **gobbled** it down.

He continued wandering along the hallway, enjoying the lovely classroom displays. He stopped to study one that he thought was especially attractive. In big lettering it said:

There was a chart of **creatures**, with a blue whale at the top and the dot of a flea at the bottom.

When Mrs. Feeny saw the principal outside her room, she invited him in. "Please join us," she said. "**Nancy** was just about to give a science presentation on an interesting creature."

Nancy hoped to be a zoologist one day, and science was her favorite subject.

"Thank you," said Mr. Bundy, stepping inside.

Nancy cleared her throat and began, "The title of my presentation is 'When Is a Worm Not a Worm?'"

"When it turns into the earth!" called Mr. Bundy, chuckling as he pictured a worm digging into dirt.

The kids groaned at the joke while Nancy waited for the principal to settle down.

"Sorry to **interrupt**," said Mr. Bundy. "Please continue."

"A worm is not a worm when it's a superworm," said Nancy.

"Does it wear a cape and save the day?" asked Mr. Bundy. He chuckled again, picturing a worm in a superhero cape.

This time the kids laughed too while Nancy waited for everyone to settle down.

"Sorry again," said Mr. Bundy. "Please continue."

Nancy went on to explain that the superworm is an important stage in the **emergence** of a darkling beetle.

"Think of a caterpillar before the butterfly comes," said Nancy. "I feed superworms to my pet lizards and brought some to show you."

Before she had a chance to open the container, Mr. Bundy jumped up to leave so he wouldn't have to see any worms that weren't worms.

SUPERWORM

"That was a super report! In fact, it was super-duper!" he said.

"Thank you, Mr. Bundy," said Nancy. She studied him with her scientist's powers of **observation**. Aside from being unusually goofy this morning, there was a little something about him that didn't look right. She couldn't put her finger on what it was, but she was **determined** to figure it out before the day was through.

When she got back to her seat, she whispered to Roger and **Hector**, "There's something odd about the way Mr. Bundy looks today."

"There's a lot that's odd about him today," said Hector. "He must have had goofy flakes for breakfast."

"I can't figure out what's going on," said Roger. "It isn't April Fools' Day. I bet he has a plan, and I bet it's something good."

3

Bzzz!

Mr. Bundy wandered into **Ms. Tilly**'s room next. He knocked on the door and poked his head in.

The students all said, **"Good morning, Mr. Bundy!"**

"Welcome to our class," said

Ms. Tilly. "It's our music time, and we were just about to sing a favorite funny song."

"I love funny songs!" said Mr. Bundy.

He went in and pulled up a chair.

Ms. Tilly and her class began to sing:

*"I know an old lady who
swallowed a fly.
I don't know why
she swallowed the fly.
Perhaps she'll die.*

*"I know an old lady who
swallowed a spider
that wriggled and jiggled
and tickled inside her.
She swallowed the spider
to catch the fly. . . ."*

Just then Mr. Bundy heard a fly buzzing overhead. **Bzzz.**

Uh-oh! Mr. Bundy's mind started buzzing too. *What if one of these sweet little children tries to swallow that fly! Then the child will want to swallow a spider, and then . . . and then . . .*

He couldn't even finish the thought.

Mr. Bundy jumped up to catch the fly. ***Bzzz.*** He leaped over chairs. He leaped over children. ***Bzzz! Bzzz!***

"Everyone, close your mouths!" he called.

The children were laughing too hard to keep their mouths closed.

"It's okay, Mr. Bundy! It's just a fly!" said Ms. Tilly.

But Mr. Bundy wasn't listening.

The fly was heading for the door and so was he. They both flew out of the room and down the hall.

If Mr. Bundy had his way, it would soon be "Bye-bye, fly."

4

Something's Up

Hector was on his way back from a bathroom break and had stopped to get a drink at the water fountain.

"**Quick!** Hector, close your mouth!" called Mr. Bundy.

Hector closed his mouth so

fast, a **gush** of water splashed right into his face.

The next thing he saw was Mr. Bundy racing this way and that, wildly waving his arms. When the principal got to the school's front door, he quickly opened, then closed it.

"And don't come back!" yelled Mr. Bundy.

Hector stared at him in **disbelief**. Who was the principal talking to? And why did he suddenly look so happy? Mr. Bundy was pumping

his fists in the air, shouting, **"Yes! Yes!"** as if his favorite team had just won a big game.

Goofy flakes for sure, thought Hector. He hurried back to his classroom and slipped into his seat.

"Pssst!" Hector whispered to his friends. "Mr. Bundy's definitely not himself today. I think Marty Q. Marvel performed some kind of magic trick. Maybe he turned himself into Mr. Bundy!"

Marty Q. Marvel was the very nice but very bumbling magician who had visited the school on several occasions.

"I don't think Marty could pull off that switcheroo," said Nancy.

"I wonder if that mischief-maker
Anansi is back."

Anansi, the tricky spider, had
once showed up at school looking like a man. He'd made Mr.

Bundy, Ms. Moore and some of the teachers disappear.

"It can't be Anansi again," said Roger. "He was **banished** from our school forever."

"Roger, Hector and Nancy, I hope you've had a very nice conversation," said Mrs. Feeny. "Now it's time to exercise more than your lips. We need to get to the gym."

"We'll have to **solve** this mystery later," whispered Roger as they all headed out.

5

An Unusual Day

After chasing the fly, Mr. Bundy was quite overheated. So instead of visiting more classrooms, he went back to the office and opened the window wide to cool himself off.

Whoosh! A strong breeze blew in. It felt great, but sent papers **swirling** every which way. It was a paper tornado! But that wasn't the worst part.

The fly was back! ***Bzzz. Bzzz.*** It had flown in through the open window. Mr. Bundy chased it around the office till it finally flew back out.

"And don't come back!" he shouted as he shut the window.

Mr. Bundy started picking things up and placing them on the desk.

That's when he noticed the tiny lettering on the calendar that said *HOODIE-HOO DAY.*

He had no idea what that was, so he turned on the computer to find out.

HOODIE-HOO DAY

WHEN IT IS:

February 20 in the Northern Hemisphere.

WHAT IT IS:

A day to chase away winter blues and feel ready for spring.

HOW TO CELEBRATE:

At noon, go outside, raise your arms and yell, "Hoodie-hoo!"

That sounds like fun, thought Mr. Bundy. He looked at his watch. It was almost noon! Quickly, he turned on the microphone.

"Goooood almost-afternoon, PS 88, and happy Hoodie-Hoo Day!" he said.

"Hoodie what?" said Roger.

"Not 'hoodie what,'" said Nancy. "He said 'hoodie who.'"

"That's a hoodie hoot," said Hector.

"Drop whatever you're doing and meet me in the schoolyard," said Mr. Bundy.

"Our emergency drills aren't usually like this," said Hector.

"Nothing about this day is like it usually is," said Roger.

"No talking, please," said Ms. Bly. "Run and get your jackets, then head out to the schoolyard. I'm sure Mr. Bundy will tell us all we need to know when we get there."

A Big Surprise

When they had gathered outside, Mr. Bundy said, "Everyone, raise your arms up to the sky and yell 'Hoodie-hoo!'"

Mr. Bundy followed his own instructions. No one else did.

"Come on, everyone!" said Mr. Bundy. **"Arms up and yell 'Hoodie-hoo!'"**

"Hoodie-hoo," they said softly.

"You can do better than that," said Mr. Bundy. "Shout it with lots of spirit and arms held high!"

"Hoodie-hoo," they all said a little more loudly, with arms inching upward.

A few kids began to giggle. This was starting to be fun.

"Now give it all you've got," said Mr. Bundy. "We need to chase away the winter blues and feel ready for spring."

The whole school raised their arms high in the air and shouted, **"HOODIE-HOO!"** as loudly as they could.

They thought they had done a very good job, so they were surprised to see Mr. Bundy standing with his hands on his hips, looking **befuddled**.

But wait. It wasn't the same Mr. Bundy. There were *two* Mr. Bundys standing side by side. The teachers and kids did **double takes**. They rubbed their eyes.

Seeing the two Mr. Bundys, Ms. Moore almost fainted.

"Barnaby!" said one Mr. Bundy happily.

"Benny," said the other Mr. Bundy sternly.

"What in the world is going on?" said Ms. Moore, pulling herself together.

7

Hoodie-Hoo!

"You're twins!" said Roger.

"Yes, we are," said Benny and Barnaby Bundy together.

"You're **identical** twins," said Nancy.

She studied them with her

scientist's eye, again noticing an odd little something about Benny. Then she figured it out. Benny's hair was parted on his left side. These days, Principal Bundy parted his hair on the right. Mystery solved.

"Please tell me what you're doing here, Benny," said the real Principal Bundy.

"I was trying to help you," said Benny. "Yesterday when I came to visit, you looked very tired. I thought you needed an extra day off, but I knew you wouldn't take one. So when you weren't looking, I slipped into your room, turned off your alarm, and changed your calendar so you'd think today was Sunday. I didn't expect anyone at school to notice that it was me instead of you, since we look exactly alike."

"Oh, we noticed," said Hector. Everyone laughed.

"How did you find out that you'd been tricked, Mr. Bundy?" asked Roger.

"I saw it was Monday when I started reading the news," said

the principal. "Then, when I saw that my bike and my best suit were gone, I knew I'd better get right over here."

"I'm glad you got here in time to celebrate Hoodie-Hoo Day with us," said Benny to his brother.

"What's all this hoodie hooey?" asked Principal Bundy.

"February twentieth is the Hoodie-Hoo holiday. I saw it on your calendar. It's for chasing away the winter blues," said Benny.

"That sounds nice," said Mr. Bundy. "But today is *January* twentieth . . . not February twentieth."

"What do you mean? How could that be?" said Benny.

Then he remembered the papers swirling around the office when he'd opened the window. The wind must have blown the calendar from January to February.

Benny looked down in the dumps.

"I'm such a noodlehead!"

"Don't feel bad," said Principal Bundy. "We're all noodleheads sometimes. You have a really good heart. That's what counts."

"And we had a super-duper day!" said Nancy.

A month later, when it really *was* February twentieth, Benny Bundy was back at PS 88. Just before noon, he led everyone outside and said, "You all know what to do!"

The whole school knew exactly what to do.

Together they raised their arms up to the sky and shouted with spirit, "Hoodie-hoo!"

And they chased the blues away.

Word List

banished (BA•nishd): Sent away forever, as punishment

befuddled (bih•FUH•duld): Completely confused or puzzled

behavior (bee•HAY•vyer): The way someone acts

creatures (KREE•churz): Any living beings

determined (dih•TER•mund): Firmly set to do something

disbelief (dis•buh•LEEF): The act of not believing something

double takes (DUH•buhl TAYKS): Second looks of surprise when it's hard to believe what's been seen

emergence (ih•MER•jents): The act of coming into being or into view

gobbled (GAH•buld): Ate quickly

gush (GUSH): A sudden, strong flow

identical (eye•DEN•tih•kuhl): Exactly the same

interrupt (in•tuh•RUPT): To break into something that's in progress

observation (ahb•zer•VAY•shun):
Getting knowledge by carefully
considering what one is seeing

solve (SAHLV): To find an
explanation for

swirling (SWER•ling): Moving
quickly in a twisting, circling
motion

Questions

1. Noodlehead stories are about people who do goofy things. Don't we all! What's the last goofy thing *you* did?

2. Would you like to write a noodlehead story? What will you name your noodlehead character?

3. "Trading places" stories are told all around the world. Who would you like to trade places with?

4. Hoodie-Hoo Day is for chasing away the winter blues. When you have the blues, what do you do to chase them away?

5. Did you notice that one person was left off the Cast of Characters list at the beginning of the book? Who is it, and why do you think that character wasn't included?